THE
FATE
OF
FAUSTO

A PAINTED FABLE

BY OLIVER JEFFERS

PHILOMEL

To Kurt and Joe
(and the rest)

There was once a man who believed he owned everything

and set out to survey
what was his.

"You are mine,"

said Fausto to the flower.

"Yes,"
said the flower.
"I am yours."

Content,
Fausto walked on.

"You are mine,"
he said to the sheep.

"Yes,"
said the sheep.
"I suppose I am."

Feeling satisfied,

Fausto walked on.

Next Fausto came upon
a tree and declared,
"Tree, you are mine."

To which the tree replied,
"Oh, all right,
I can be yours."

And the tree bowed
before the man.

This pleased Fausto,
and he walked on,
happy to be owning

a sheep
and a flower
and his tree.

Before long, Fausto had claimed a field and a forest and a lake.

At first, the lake had pretended
not to hear,

but Fausto showed that lake

who was boss.

When he reached a mountain,
Fausto said in a clear voice,

"Mountain, you are mine!"

"No," said the mountain.

"I am my own."

This angered Fausto,
and he stamped his foot
and made a fist.

Still the mountain
would not move.

But Fausto put up such a fight
you would not believe,
and showed the mountain
who was boss.

Eventually,

the mountain bowed before
Fausto and said,

"Yes. You are in charge.
I am yours."

Feeling very important,
Fausto easily conquered
a boat to set off to sea.

For a mountain, a lake,
a forest, a field, a tree,
a sheep, and a flower
were not enough for him.

When he had gotten
far enough from shore,
Fausto said in a loud voice,

"Sea, you are mine."

But the sea

was silent.

"You belong to me, sea.
I know you can hear me,"

said Fausto, louder still.

Then, after a while,

the sea said quietly,

"You do not own me."

"You are wrong. I do," Fausto replied,

unsure which way to look,
for the voice appeared to
come from everywhere.

"But you do not even love me," said the sea.

"You are wrong again,"
said the man.
"I love you very much."

But Fausto was lying,

and the sea knew it.

"How can you love me when you do not understand me?"
the sea asked Fausto.

"You are wrong a third time," said Fausto.

"I understand you deeply."
Then added, feeling impatient,
"Now, admit you are mine,
or I will show you who is boss."

"And how will you do that?"
asked the sea.

"I will stamp
my foot
and make
a fist."

"If you wish to
stamp your foot,
then come show me
how it is done
so I understand."

And, in order to show
his anger and importance,

Fausto climbed overboard

to stamp his foot on the sea.

But he did not understand.

And he did not know
how to swim.

The sea was sad for him,

but carried on being the sea.

The mountain, too,
went back to its business.

And the lake and the forest,
the field and the tree,
the sheep and the flower

carried on as before.

For the fate of Fausto

did not matter to them.

JOE HELLER

True story, Word of Honor:
Joseph Heller, an important and funny writer
now dead,
and I were at a party given by a billionaire
on Shelter Island.
I said, "Joe, how does it make you feel
to know that our host only yesterday
may have made more money
than your novel 'Catch-22'
has earned in its entire history?"
And Joe said, "I've got something he can never have."
And I said, "What on earth could that be, Joe?"
And Joe said, "The knowledge that I've got enough."
Not bad! Rest in peace!

Kurt Vonnegut
The New Yorker, May 16, 2005

Philomel Books
An imprint of Penguin Random House LLC, New York

This story was written by Oliver Jeffers in 2015.

The art for this book was made at Idem Press in Paris using
a manual lithography press during the summer of 2018.

First American edition published by Philomel Books,
an imprint of Penguin Random House LLC, 2019.
First published in Great Britain by HarperCollins *Children's Books* in 2019.

Visit us online at penguinrandomhouse.com

Library of Congress Cataloguing-in-Publication Data is available upon request

Design by Rory Jeffers and David Pearson.
Typeset in Chambord Maigre (Fonderie Olive, 1945).
Marbling for endpapers made by Jemma Lewis.
With special thanks to Hayley Nichols,
and to Maï Saikusa and Martin Giffard of Idem Press.

Manufactured in Italy

ISBN: 9780593115015

10 9 8 7 6 5 4 3 2 1